Tony Johnston
The Last Snow of Winter

pictures by Friso Henstra

TAMBOURINE BOOKS  NEW YORK

94 09154

Text copyright © 1993 by Tony Johnston
Illustrations copyright © 1993 by Friso Henstra

All rights reserved. No part of this book may be reproduced or
utilized in any form or by any means, electronic or mechanical,
including photocopying, recording, or by any information storage
or retrieval system, without permission in writing from the
Publisher. Inquiries should be addressed to
Tambourine Books, a division of William Morrow & Company, Inc.,
1350 Avenue of the Americas, New York, New York 10019.
The illustrations were painted with watercolor and ink on paper.
Printed in the United States of America.

Library of Congress Cataloging in Publication Data

Johnston, Tony. The last snow of winter/by Tony Johnston;
pictures by Friso Henstra. p. cm.
Summary: The great sculptor Gaston Pompicard creates a snow
sculpture for his friends the children, and then later he
receives a similar gift from them during the last snow of winter.
[1. Snow sculpture—Fiction. 2. Winter—Fiction.] I. Henstra,
Friso, ill. II. Title.
PZ7.J6478Las 1993 [E]—dc20 92-33862 CIP AC
ISBN 0-688-10749-4 (trade).—ISBN 0-688-10750-8 (lib. bdg.).

10 9 8 7 6 5 4 3 2 1
First edition

CENTRAL ARKANSAS LIBRARY SYSTEM
LITTLE ROCK PUBLIC LIBRARY
700 LOUISIANA STREET
LITTLE ROCK, ARKANSAS 72201

In memory of Madame Louisette de L'Arbre d'Estaing
   T.J.

To Rietje
   F.H.

All was quiet in the little French town. The lights in the houses were out for the night. The children were sleeping. The stars were winking.

In a small house an old gentleman was asleep. It was Gaston Pompicard, the sculptor. Once he had sculpted for kings.

He slept soundly. He snored soundly. At his bedside his dog, Louisette, also slept and snored.

When the night was quietest of all, Gaston Pompicard
heard a sound. What could it be? A thief?

It was the sound of falling snow.

The first snow of winter, he thought.

He went to the window to see.

The snow fell thickly. It clung to branches and bark, turning the trees to lace. It piled up on doorsteps and bicycles. It whitened the land.

He had a grand idea.

Quickly, he put on his work clothes. Then overcoat, muffler, and beret. All red, his favorite color. He collected his tools. And a blanket.

Gaston Pompicard went to his little kitchen. He heated pea soup for himself and Louisette. It would be cold outside. They should be warm inside.

He opened the door. He and Louisette stood for a
moment in the new snow, feeling it fall down upon them.
He ate a snowflake and smiled.
Now he was ready to work.
Stars and street lamps lit the snow.

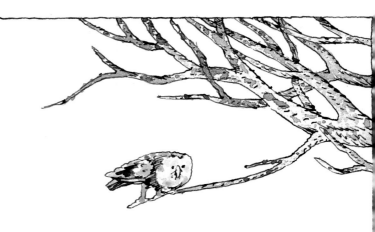

Gaston Pompicard looked for the right place to work.
He saw a patch of snowy ground beneath a chestnut tree.
Ah. There.

He flapped the blanket up, then let it settle to the
ground. Louisette settled herself upon it.

Then the old man began to work. He piled snow into
large mounds. He shaped it. And molded it. He patted and
pressed it.

Then he scooped it and chiseled it and gouged it and rasped it with his tools. Last of all he spread snow over everything with a putty knife, as if icing a cake.

Now he was done.

Not quite. Gaston Pompicard went into his house. He brought something back. He put it on his sculpture.

Voilà! He ate a snowflake and smiled. There! "A sculptor for kings is a fine thing to be. But a sculptor for friends is finer."

He and Louisette went back to bed.

The sun came out. The children came out. They ran laughing and shouting in the snow.

When they saw the sculpture, they laughed and shouted louder still.

"Look," they cried. "It is us! *Merci,* Monsieur Pompicard! Thank you! *Merci! Merci! Merci!*"

All winter the snow fell. All winter it was beautiful. Gaston Pompicard and Louisette enjoyed it every day. They walked where no one else had walked. They left footprints, both large and small.

Every day they watched the children play. Sometimes they saw birds fighting for seeds. Sometimes they watched squirrels seeking nuts. Then Gaston Pompicard bought hot bread from the baker. He gave some to the birds. He gave some to the squirrels. He gave some to Louisette. He gave some to himself. He ate some snowflakes too.

One day he did not go out in the snow. He stayed in bed.
He was sick.
He sneezed and sneezed.
"Acheee! Achooo!"
Louisette did not sneeze. But she slept on his bed to keep
him company. She stayed there for many days.

Spring flowers were already spiking up. Icicles thawed and dripped. Birds were returning from far away.

Outside, the old man heard the children playing. He felt a little better.

Suddenly everything got *very* quiet. He didn't
hear the children. He didn't hear anything except
his own sneezes.

When it was quietest of all, he heard a sound.
What could it be? A thief?

It was the sound of falling snow.

The last snow of winter, he thought.

But he felt too tired to watch it.

He heard another sound. What could *that* be?

It was the sound of whispers and giggles.

He went to the window to see.

"Look, Louisette!" he cried. "It is us! *Merci, mes amis.*
Thank you, my friends. *Merci! Merci! Merci!*"

Gaston Pompicard felt much better.

"It is cold outside," he told the children. "Come in,
please."

He heated pea soup.

Soon everyone felt warm and happy, eating
soup and watching the last snow of winter.